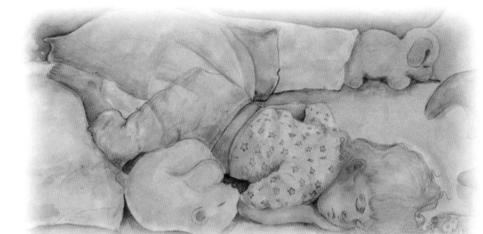

To the Moon and Back

Written by Randi M. Hull
Illustrated by Sarah Anne Reganis

D1383372

Puddle Creek Books
an imprint of Wyatt-MacKenzie

Puddle Creek Books
an imprint of Wyatt-MacKenzie

To the Moon and Back by Randi M. Hull

ISBN 978-1-438203-61-4

S E C O N D   E D I T I O N

Puddle Creek Books, an imprint of Wyatt-MacKenzie

Imprint information www.wymacpublishing.com

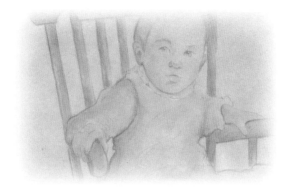

For my mother.
And for the two most wonderful children in the world.
I love you to the moon and back
~ R.H.

A young mother watched as her beautiful baby daughter played in the early morning sunlight. As if sensing her, the baby gazed thoughtfully; her blue-green eyes catching just a small glint of the sun.

The mother thought, *will my daughter ever know just how much I love her?*

That evening, the mother rocked her bouncing baby under a starry sky and a smiling moon. "My darling," she whispered. "I love you to the moon and back."

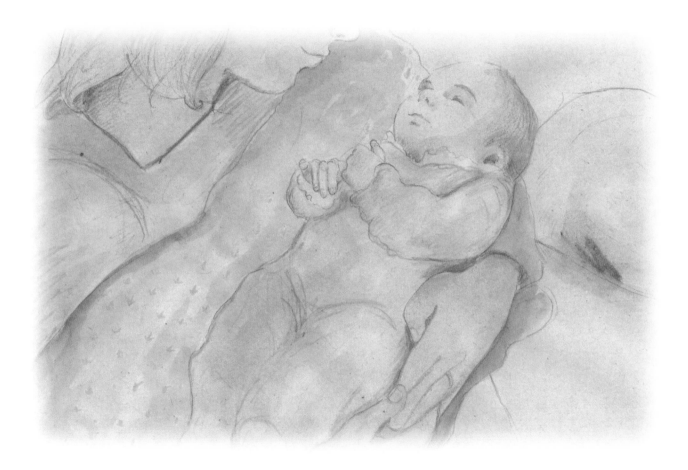

And she laid down her precious bundle as if she were wrapped in the most delicate silk.

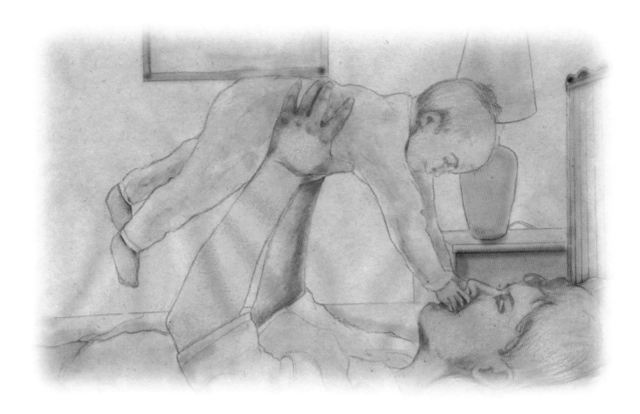

The years passed as if they were minutes, each one quicker than the last.

The young mother rose one morning to find her pretty little five year old daughter dancing in the sunlight streaming through a nearby window. She stood back and watched her happy little girl with the golden curls and rosy cheeks. Twirl after twirl…..

And she thought to herself, *will my daughter ever know just how much I love her?*

That evening, as she tucked in her little ballerina under a starry sky and a smiling moon, she whispered, "My darling," "I love you to the moon and back."

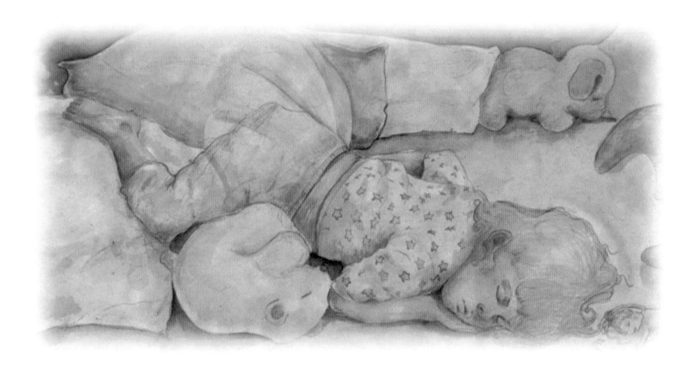

And just as before, the years passed as if they were minutes, each one quicker than the last.

The mother awoke one morning to the wonderful scent of crisp, fresh roses mixed with singing birds and bright sunshine. She gazed out of her window to find her lovely young daughter walking through the garden.

The girl stopped to admire each rose thoughtfully, as if she were seeing it's sunkissed beauty for the first time. Sensing that she was being watched, the young girl glanced up at her mother with a mischievous grin, and just a glint of sunlight in her eyes.

The mother wondered, *will my daughter ever know just how much I love her?*

That evening, she wrapped that beautiful girl with the golden curls in her arms. Under a starry sky and a smiling moon, she softly whispered, "My darling," "I love you to the moon and back."

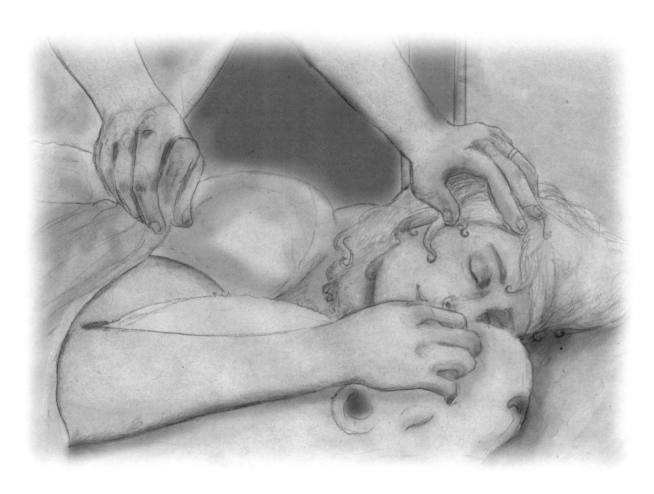

The years passed ever so quickly, as if they were minutes, each one just a bit quicker than the last.

The mother awoke on this, the best morning with the sun gleaming like it were painted just for her. Outside, she found her happy smiling baby, nervously pacing in her graduation gown. She stopped to gaze at the curious, bubbly little girl who was now a golden-haired young woman.

The mother brushed away a single tear. *Will my daughter ever know just how much I love her?*

That evening, the mother stood next to the window under a starry sky and a smiling moon. She thought back to the bouncing baby ballerina with the mischievous grin once more. Softly she whispered, "My darling," "I love you to the moon and back."

Behind her, she turned to see her beautiful daughter, with a brilliant sparkle in her eye like that of a brightly shining star.

"Mother," she smiled. "I know."

Made in the USA
San Bernardino, CA
04 June 2013